D1571283

A Note to Parents and Caregivers:

With a focus on math, science, and social studies, *Read-it!* Readers support both the learning of content information and the extension of more complex reading skills. They encourage the development of problem-solving skills that help children expand their thinking.

 The PURPLE LEVEL presents basic topics and objects using high frequency words and simple language patterns.

 The RED LEVEL presents familiar topics using common words and repeating sentence patterns.

 The BLUE LEVEL presents new ideas using a larger vocabulary and varied sentence structure.

 The YELLOW LEVEL presents more challenging ideas, a broad vocabulary, and wide variety in sentence structure.

 The GREEN LEVEL presents more complex ideas, an extended vocabulary range, and expanded language structures.

 The ORANGE LEVEL presents a wide range of ideas and concepts using challenging vocabulary and complex language structures.

When sharing a content focused book with your child, read to find out facts and concepts, pausing often to restate and talk about the new information. The realistic story format provides an opportunity to talk about the language used, and to learn about reading to problem-solve for information. Encourage children to measure, make maps, and consider other situations that allow them to apply what they are learning.

There is no right or wrong way to share books with children. Find time to read and share new learning with your child, and pass on the legacy of literacy.

Adria F. Klein, Ph.D.
Professor Emeritus
California State University
San Bernardino, California

Editor: Julie Gassman
Designer: Hilary Wacholz
Art Director: Heather Kindseth
Managing Editor: Christianne Jones
The illustrations in this book were created with acrylic and ink.

Picture Window Books
151 Good Counsel Drive
P.O. Box 669
Mankato, MN 56002-0669
877-845-8392
www.picturewindowbooks.com

Library of Congress Cataloging-in-Publication Data
Dokas, Dara, 1968–
Saving Shadow/ by Dara Dokas ; illustrated by Evelyne Duverne.
p. cm. — (Read-it! readers. Character education)
ISBN 978-1-4048-5237-2
[1. Cats—Fiction. 2. Pets—Fiction. 3. Responsibility—Fiction.]
I. Duverne, Evelyne, 1981- ill. II. Title.
PZ7.D697427Sav 2009
[E]—dc22
                                        2008031795

Saving Shadow

by Dara Dokas
illustrated by Evelyne Duverne

Special thanks to our advisers for their expertise:

Kay A. Augustine, ED.S.
National Character Development Trainer and Consultant

Adria F. Klein, Ph.D.
Professor Emeritus, California State University
San Bernardino, California

PiCTURE WiNDOW BOOKS
Minneapolis, Minnesota

Taylor loved cats. She wanted a cat of
her own. But her mom always said, "No
pets right now."

One day, Taylor heard a quiet sound outside her house.

"Meow."

"A cat!" said Taylor.

"Kitty, where are you?" asked Taylor.
Taylor looked in the bushes.

Taylor looked under the pine tree.

Taylor looked under her porch.
She saw a small gray cat with white paws.
   "Here Kitty," said Taylor.
The cat limped away.
Something was wrong.

"Is your leg hurt?" asked Taylor. "Come out. I'll take care of you."

But the cat stayed under the porch.

Taylor sat down on the ground. "You need a name," she said. "I will call you Shadow."

Taylor tried to get Shadow to come out from under the porch. She called to Shadow. She waved a feather.

She even dangled her shoelace.
But Shadow would not move.

Taylor's mom walked out of the house. "Who are you talking to?" she asked.

"There is a cat under our porch," said Taylor. "She looks hurt."

Her mom bent down. "How do you know she is hurt?" she asked.

"I saw her limping," said Taylor.

14

"Who does she belong to?" asked Mom.
"I don't know," said Taylor. "I don't think Shadow has a home."

"Who is Shadow?" asked Mom.
"That is her name," said Taylor.

"I think Shadow needs someone to care for her," said Mom.

"What can we do?" asked Taylor.

"We can bring her to a veterinarian," said Mom. "But first we need to catch her."

16

"I know!" said Taylor. "The Garcias have a pet carrier."

"And if we put some tuna fish inside it, Shadow might come out," said Mom.

Taylor's mom went inside to get a plate of tuna. Taylor ran next door to the Garcias' house. Mr. Garcia and his son brought over their carrier.

"That is a pretty cat," said Mr. Garcia.
"Are you going to keep her?"

"No," said Mom. "No pets right now."

Mr. Garcia set up the pet carrier. Taylor put the tuna inside. They all backed away from the porch.

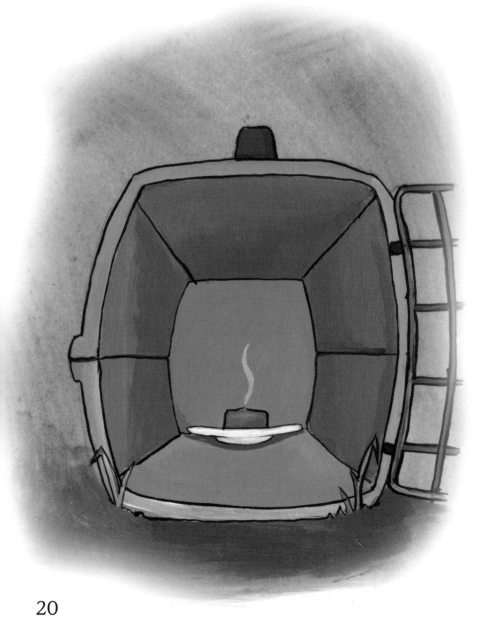

Shadow slowly walked out. She sniffed the carrier. Then, she walked inside.

Mom quickly shut the door. Shadow looked surprised, but she was quiet and ate the tuna.

Taylor and her mother took Shadow to the veterinarian. The veterinarian cleaned Shadow. She put a bandage on Shadow's hurt foot.

Taylor and her mom brought Shadow home.
Taylor carefully lifted Shadow out of the cage.

Shadow sat on the couch. She curled into a ball. Taylor sat down next to Shadow. She gently pet Shadow's fur to comfort her. The cat purred.

"She likes it here," said Taylor.
"She looks happy," said Mom. "But we
need to find out if she belongs to anyone."

Taylor and her mother put up 'Found Cat' signs all around the neighborhood. They called the animal shelter. No one was missing a cat like Shadow.

Taylor took care
of Shadow.
She fed her.

She brushed her.

She helped clean
the litter box.

After two weeks, Mom said, "No one has called. I don't think Shadow has a home."

"Shadow needs someone to take care of her," said Taylor.

Mom thought about how Taylor had cared for Shadow. Taylor had fed, brushed, and cleaned up after her.

"You showed me that you can take care of an animal. I think we can keep her," Mom said.

"You belong to us! We are your family now!" Taylor said as she hugged Shadow.

"Meow!" said Shadow. She was happy to be home.

30

Caring Activity

There are many ways to show you care about other people or things. Animals especially need people to care for them. They often depend on people for food or shelter.

Here are two ways you can help care for animals, even if you don't have a pet.

1. Volunteer at your local animal shelter. Shelters often need volunteers to hold and brush the cats and walk the dogs. Invite a grown-up to do this activity with you.
2. Organize a donation drive to collect cat and dog food, cat litter, animal beds, toys, and money for your local animal shelter. You can call the shelter to see if they need other things as well. The people (and animals) at the shelter will love these donations.

Glossary

belong—to be owned by someone
care—to make sure someone or something is safe and happy
comfort—to make someone or something feel better
veterinarian—a doctor for animals

To Learn More

More Books to Read

Graham, Bob. *"Let's Get a Pup!" said Kate.* Cambridge, Mass.:
  Candlewick Press, 2001.
Small, Mary. *Caring: A Book About Caring.* Minneapolis:
  Picture Window Books, 2006.
Wickstrom, Silvie. *I Love You, Mister Bear.* New York:
  HarperCollins, 2003.

On the Web

FactHound offers a safe, fun way to find Web sites related to
topics in this book. All of the sites on FactHound have been
researched by our staff.

1. Visit *www.facthound.com*
2. Type in this special code: 1404852379
3. Click on the FETCH IT button.

Your trusty FactHound will fetch the best sites for you!

Look for all the books in the *Read-it!* Readers: Character Education series:

Dirty Gertie (responsibility)
Fair Game (fairness)
Green Park (citizenship)
Rocky Recess (respect)
Rules of the Net (trustworthiness)
Saving Shadow (caring)

HUNTSVILLE PUBLIC LIBRARY

5 1216 03014118

HUNTSVILLE PUBLIC LIBRARY
1216 14TH STREET
HUNTSVILLE TX 77340

OVERDUE FINE 10 CENTS PER DAY